For the humpbacks who healed my heart
— KP

For my mom and dad, who believed in
me enough to hang all of my drawings on
the refrigerator (even the really bad ones)
— CS

Published in 2023 by Groundwood Books / House of Anansi Press
groundwoodbooks.com

We gratefully acknowledge for their financial support of our publishing
program the Canada Council for the Arts, the Ontario Arts Council and the
Government of Canada.

 Canada Council   Conseil des Arts
for the Arts   du Canada

 ONTARIO ARTS COUNCIL
CONSEIL DES ARTS DE L'ONTARIO
an Ontario government agency
un organisme du gouvernement de l'Ontario

With the participation of the Government of Canada   Canadä
Avec la participation du gouvernement du Canada

Library and Archives Canada Cataloguing in Publication
Title: Maybe a whale / story by Kirsten Pendreigh ; pictures by Crystal Smith.
Names: Pendreigh, Kirsten, author. | Smith, Crystal (Artist), illustrator.
Identifiers: Canadiana (print) 20220449147 | Canadiana (ebook)
20220449163 | ISBN 9781773066646 (hardcover) | ISBN 9781773066653
(EPUB) | ISBN 9781773066660 (Kindle)
Subjects: LCGFT: Picture books. | LCGFT: Fiction.
Classification: LCC PS8631.E533 M39 2023 | DDC jC813/.6—dc23

The illustrations were created with digital paint and layered textures.
Edited by Emma Sakamoto
Designed by Michael Solomon and Lucia Kim
Printed and bound in South Korea

MAYBE A WHALE

WORDS BY

KIRSTEN PENDREIGH

PICTURES BY

CRYSTAL SMITH

GROUNDWOOD BOOKS

HOUSE OF ANANSI PRESS

TORONTO / BERKELEY

After,
    Mom shows me the note Grandpa left,
        with maps for my first ocean trip.
    Grandpa was always talking about the sea
        and his whales.
    He was supposed to take me to see them.

Mom says the trip will do us good.
I don't think she's right.
Grandpa won't be there.

We pack food and water, drive for days.
I stare out the window.

The ocean appears.
*How could you find a whale
in all that water?*

We rent a kayak, stuff our clothes
    in waterproof bags.
Fold, roll, *click!*
Shove them into hatches — *thunk!*

I squeeze on scratchy water shoes,
    heavy rubber pants,
    a lifejacket that hugs me tight.
Like Grandpa did.
And we're off.

It's windy and the waves have white tips.
Salt spray wakes my face.
*Could a whale be swimming
    underneath us …?*
We paddle hard to reach small islands,
    coves where the water is calm.

Moon jellies bob beside us,
   anemones flutter hello below.
A seal slips past, rolls to watch me
   with dark eyes.

We squeak over bull kelp,
   scrape onto sand,
   unload our weight
   and lift the kayak above the tide line.

Mom helps me light the stove for noodles.
Later, we'll make hot chocolate
    with the noodle water.
I watch for whales.
Maybe they're sleeping ...

We unfold tent poles. *Click, click, snap.*
Thread them through. *Pop. Pop.*
I used to camp with Grandpa in our backyard.
Here the sand is loose,
    so we weigh down the tabs with rocks.
"We don't want to blow away in the night,"
    Mom laughs.
I haven't heard her laugh in a long time.
"Or slide into the sea," I joke.

We build our fire close to shore,
toast marshmallows.
Sparks hiss as they hit dark water.
There's no moon, but millions of
stars shine above.

Why are there more stars here?
Is Grandpa up there?
Can whales see stars?
Are the whales even here?

We rinse sticky hands in salty water.
Our splashes light up!
"Bioluminescence," Mom tells me.
Living light!

"I wish Grandpa were here," I say. "I wish I'd
     seen a whale."
"Maybe tomorrow."
Mom tells me about the first whale she saw
     with Grandpa.
How it rose up and slapped *Hello!* with its tail.

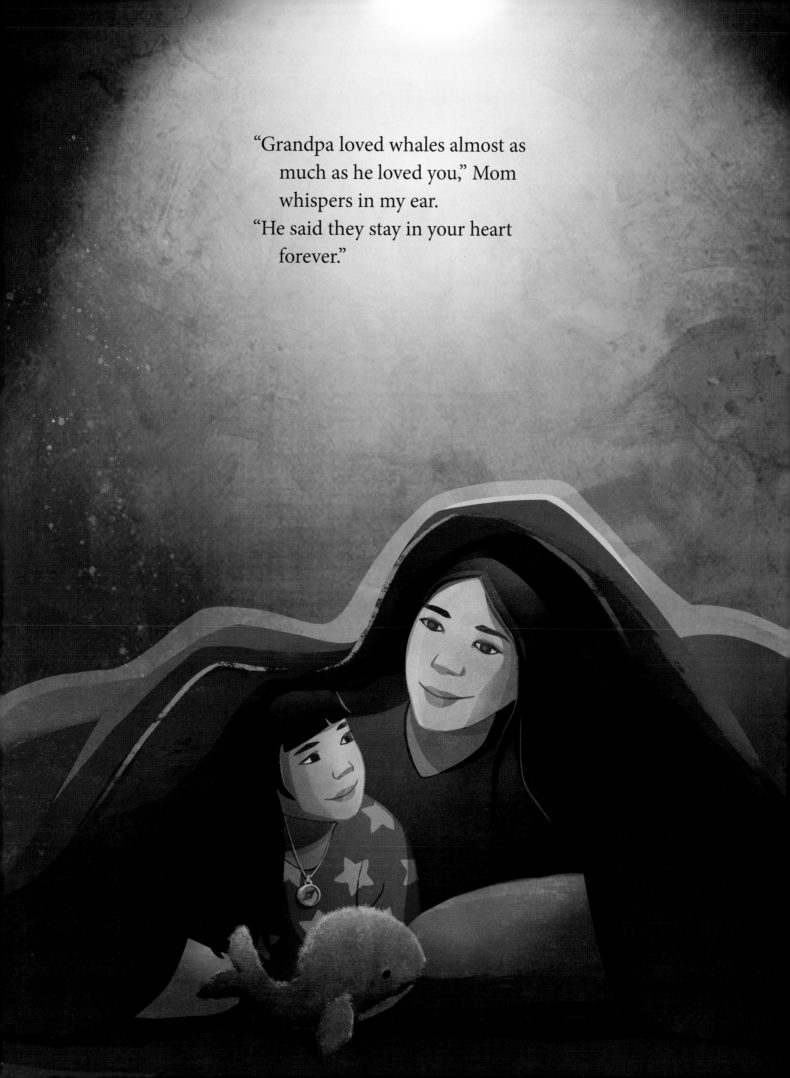

"Grandpa loved whales almost as much as he loved you," Mom whispers in my ear.
"He said they stay in your heart forever."

It's so quiet, we can hear
leaves rustle in the forest,
waves lap-lapping,
and then, a new sound —

Pushhhhh!
— coming from the ocean.
Pushhhhh!
Louder! And closer!

"It's the whales!" says Mom.
"Humpbacks! Breathing in the bay!"
We scramble to the shore, but we can't
see them in the dark.

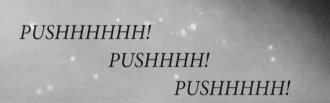

PUSHHHHHH!
    PUSHHHH!
        PUSHHHHH!

I take my own deep breath.
I hear my heart pumping.
Pushhhhhh!

I breathe with the whales.
My heart thump-thumps with them.
Pushhhhh! Pushhhhh!

Giant spray-breaths carry over calm water,
rock me to sleep.
Pushhhh. Pushhh. Pushhh.

In the morning, the only sound
is the sea lap-lapping.
We eat porridge and pack up.

Mom checks the charts and currents.
And we're off!
Scrape, sit, paddle.
Keep going.

I tell Grandpa the whales are still here.
Even if I can't see them.